CAMDEN COUNTY LIBRARY
203 LAUREL ROAD
VOORHEES, NJ 08043

S0-BNB-888

E Wyn
Wynne-Jones, Tim.
Zoom

DEC 1 0 2009

ZOOM

For Amanda Lewis — T W J

For Michael — E B

ZOOM

By Tim Wynne-Jones

Pictures by Eric Beddows

GROUNDWOOD BOOKS

HOUSE OF ANANSI PRESS

TORONTO   BERKELEY

Text copyright © 2009 by Tim Wynne-Jones
Illustrations copyright © 2009 by Eric Beddows
(*Zoom at Sea* first published in 1983; *Zoom Away*, 1985; *Zoom Upstream*, 1992)
Published in Canada and the USA in 2009 by Groundwood Books

All rights reserved. No part of this publication may be reproduced, stored in a retrieval system
or transmitted, in any form or by any means, without the prior written consent of the publisher or a
license from The Canadian Copyright Licensing Agency (Access Copyright). For an Access Copyright
license, visit www.accesscopyright.ca or call toll free to 1-800-893-5777.

Groundwood Books / House of Anansi Press
110 Spadina Avenue, Suite 801, Toronto, Ontario M5V 2K4
or c/o Publishers Group West
1700 Fourth Street, Berkeley, CA 94710

We acknowledge for their financial support of our publishing program the Canada Council for the Arts,
the Government of Canada through the Book Publishing Industry Development Program (BPIDP) and
the Ontario Arts Council.

ONTARIO ARTS COUNCIL
CONSEIL DES ARTS DE L'ONTARIO

Library and Archives Canada Cataloguing in Publication

Wynne-Jones, Tim
Zoom / Tim Wynne-Jones ; illustrations by Eric Beddows.

Contents: Zoom at sea – Zoom away – Zoom upstream.

ISBN 978-0-88899-936-8

1. Cats–Juvenile fiction. I. Beddows, Eric
II. Title. III. Title: Zoom at sea. IV. Title: Zoom upstream. V. Title: Zoom away.

PS8595.Y59Z458 2009   jC813'.54   C2009-902923-5

The illustrations were done in graphite pencil.
Cover design by Michael Solomon
Design by Alysia Shewchuk

Printed and bound in China

ZOOM AT SEA

Zoom loved water. Not to drink — he liked cream to drink — Zoom liked water to play with.

One night, when a leaky tap filled the kitchen sink, Zoom strapped wooden spoons to his feet with elastic bands and paddled in the water for hours. He loved it.

The next night he made a boat from a wicker basket with a towel for a sail. Blown around the bathtub all night, he was as happy as could be.

There was no stopping him. Every night when other self-respecting cats were out mousing and howling Zoom stayed indoors and sailed about in the dark. By day he watched the tap and dreamed.

One afternoon while dreaming in the attic he noticed a shelf he had not seen before. A dusty diary lay next to a photograph of a large yellow tomcat with white whiskers and a black sou'wester. It was inscribed: "For Zoom from Uncle Roy."

Zoom opened the diary and on the last page he found an address and a map. "The Sea and how to get there," it said.

The Sea was not far, really. Zoom took a bus. He arrived very early in the morning, at a house with a big front door. It was so early Zoom was afraid to knock but the light was on and if he listened closely he thought he could hear someone inside. With great excitement he rapped three times.

The door opened. Before him stood a large woman in a blue dress. She wore silver earrings and many silver bracelets on her wrists.

"I want to go to sea," said Zoom nervously.

The woman smiled, but said nothing. Zoom spoke louder.

"I'm Uncle Roy's nephew and I want to go to sea."

"Ahh!" said the woman, nodding her head. "Come in my little sailor."

Inside was cold and damp.

"I am Maria," said the woman. "I'm not ready just yet." The room was quiet and dark; everything was still. Far away Zoom could hear a sound like a leaky faucet.

He sat, trying to be patient, while Maria bustled around. Sometimes it was difficult to see her in the gloom, but he could hear the swish of her skirts and the tinkling of her bracelets.

The Sea was nothing like Uncle Roy had described in his diary. Zoom was sure he had made a mistake and he was just about to sneak away when Maria looked at her watch and winked.

"Now I'm ready."

And with that, she turned an enormous wheel several times to the right. The floor began to rumble and machinery began to whirr and hum. The room grew lighter and Zoom saw that it was very large.

Now Maria pushed a button and cranked a crank. Zoom could hear the sound of water rushing through the pipes. First there were only puddles but then it poured from the closets and lapped at his feet.

From rows upon rows of tiny doors Maria released sea gulls and sandpipers, pelicans and terns. From pots and cages she set free hundreds of crabs and octopi and squid who scurried this way and that across the sandy floor.

Maria laughed. Zoom laughed. This was more like it. Noise and sunlight and water, for now there was water everywhere.

Suddenly Zoom realized he could not even see the walls of this giant room. Only the sun coming up like gold, and silver fish dancing on the waves. Far away he could see a fishing boat.

Maria smiled and said, "Go on. It's all yours."

Quickly he gathered some old logs and laced them together with seaweed. He made a raft and decorated it with shells as white as Maria's teeth.

When it was ready, he pushed and he heaved with all his might and launched the raft into the waves.

"I'm at Sea!" he called.

He danced around on his driftwood deck and occasionally cupped his paws and shouted very loudly back to shore.

"More waves," or "More Sun," or "More fish."

Waves crashed against the raft. The sun beat down.
Fish leaped across the bow and frolicked in his wake.

Zoom looked back toward the shore and saw Maria. He realized, then, that he was tired. The waves subsided and the water gently began to roll toward the shore. Zoom sat and let the tide drift him back.

He sat with Maria at her little table drinking tea and eating fish fritters and watched the sun sink into the sea. As the light dimmed, the room didn't seem half so big.

Maria's bun had come undone and there was sand in the ruffles at the bottom of her dress, but still she smiled and her jewelry tinkled silver in the twilight.

"Thank you for a great day," said Zoom as he stood at the door. "May I come back?"

"I'm sure you will," said Maria.

And he did.

ZOOM AWAY

Zoom was knitting something warm. Outside, it was summer. All the other cats were in their light summer coats, chasing butterflies, rolling in the grass. But Zoom was going on an adventure.

When he had packed his supplies, Zoom took a cab to his friend Maria's house. He knocked three times on her big front door.

Maria was dressed in the fluffiest coat Zoom had ever seen.

"There's no time to lose," she said, and showed Zoom a map of the North Pole.

"I received a letter from your uncle, Captain Roy, some months ago," she said. "He was going to sail to the North Pole. He hasn't written since. Will you come with me and search for him in the High Arctic?"

"Yes," said Zoom.

"Good," said Maria.

Zoom put on his backpack and they started up the wide staircase in the front hall.

Zoom had never been upstairs at Maria's before. The way was very steep. The air grew cold. There were little hills of snow in the corners of each step. The windows on the landing were prickly with ice, and long icicles hung like teeth from the archway. The hall was carpeted with snow. Zoom put on his ping-pong paddle snowshoes.

From a dark room Zoom heard the howling of wolves.

"Owwwwwwww."

Maria suggested they sing a song so as not to be afraid.

Zoom followed Maria down corridor after corridor, from room to room. There was deep snow everywhere now.

At last Maria stopped and checked her astrolabe. "This will be a good place for lunch," she said.

They brushed the snow off two comfy chairs. Zoom placed tin cups on a frozen end table and Maria filled each one with tomato soup from a thermos bottle.

Not long after lunch they came to a narrow hall which led to a little room. There was a low door in the wall with the words "Northwest Passage" carved in wood over it. Zoom could hear the wind whistling and thumping against the other side.

He put on his goggles. Maria opened the door.

Oh, how the wind howled — louder and more ferocious than a pack of wolves.

Zoom lit his lantern. The doorway was very small. Too small for Maria.

"I'll have to find a different way," she said. "I'll meet you on the other side."

Zoom set off. It was very dark and very cold. Soon his paws were numb. Frost tugged at his whiskers.

I hope it isn't much farther, he thought.

Then he saw the light up ahead — the end of the tunnel.

Zoom scampered out into the light.

Everywhere was ice, glistening and glaring in the bright sun. The air smelled like the sea.

"Yahoo!" he cried. "The North Pole."

Zoom tied on his skates.

"Whee!" he shouted. "I'm skating on the Arctic Sea."

Round and round the wind twirled him. Gulls circled, laughing. A noisy colony of grebes crowded in close to watch. Seals barked and clapped. Zoom didn't feel cold anymore.

But after a while he got very tired. Out of breath, he clambered to the top of a frozen hill. He took out his spyglass to look around.

There was a ship stuck in the ice.

"The Catship," he read on the bow. It was Uncle Roy's boat.

It didn't take long to get there.

The ship was on an angle. It looked very lonely.

"Hello," called Zoom. There didn't seem to be anyone on board.

In the galley there was a note on the table.

To whom it may concern:
My crew and I have boarded a passing
iceberg and are heading south. We have
lots of food and water and are in a merry
mood. Be sure to give my love to Maria
and my trusty nephew Zoom if you
should meet them in your travels.
                    Yours affectionately,
                    Captain Roy.
P.S. I'll be back for the Catship when the ice
melts.

Beside the note was a captain's whistle.

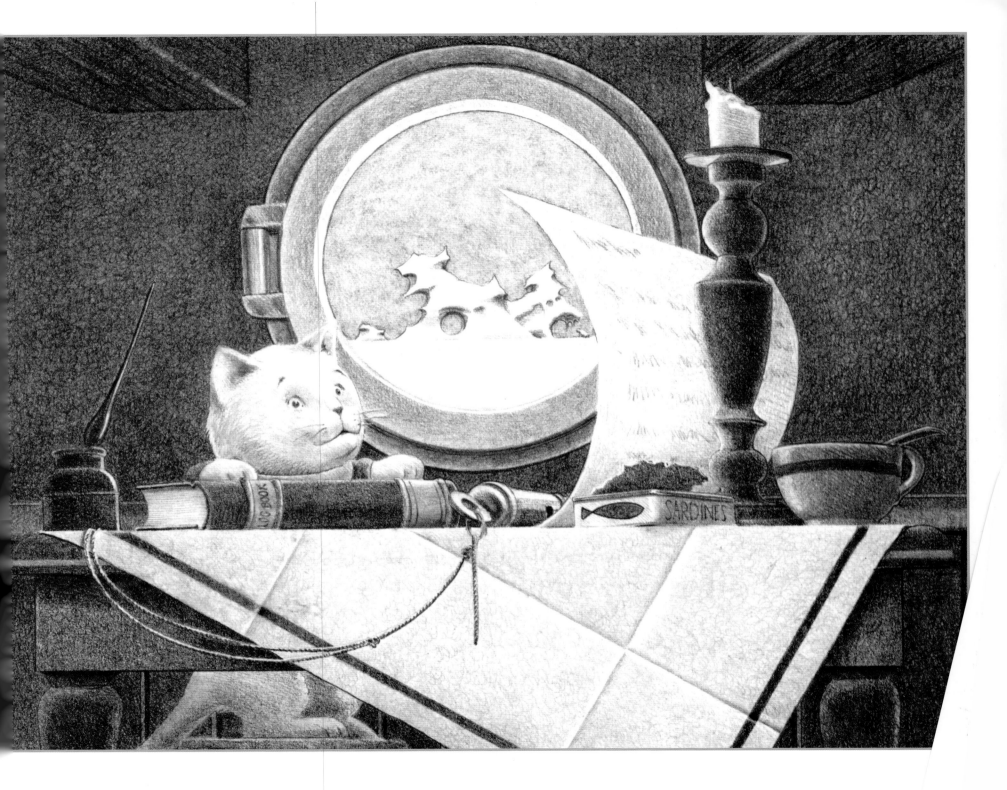

Zoom put the whistle around his neck. He looked through a porthole out at the snow. He felt sad. He had hoped to see his uncle.

"Zooooooom!" Somebody was calling his name.

It was Maria. She had made a sled out of two oars and some sailcloth.

"I'm glad to see you," said Zoom and climbed onto the sled. Then he told her about the note and the iceberg and Uncle Roy's escape.

He yawned. Maria tucked Zoom in nice and cozy.

"It's all downhill from here," she said.

Zoom drifted happily off to sleep with the arctic sun beaming down on his face.

When Zoom woke up he was curled in the wing-chair in front of the fireplace in Maria's sitting room. Maria was asleep on the chaise longue.

Zoom licked his paws and snuggled down again. He had been having a nice dream about traveling with Maria and Uncle Roy to rescue the Catship once the ice melted.

He closed his eyes.

He hoped it wouldn't be too long.

ZOOM UPSTREAM

It was fall. Zoom was visiting his friend Maria. They were in her back garden, raking leaves and planting lily bulbs for spring. Zoom pruned the roses with his very own pruning shears.

The sun was warm. Zoom stretched out on a lawn chair by the goldfish pond for a snooze.

The telephone rang.

"I'll get it," said Maria.

Zoom woke up feeling chilly. The sky had clouded over. Maria was not there. Zoom followed her muddy boot prints to the kitchen.

She had left him a hastily scribbled note.

"It's the captain. Had to go. No time to lose!"

"Uncle Roy!" thought Zoom. "What trouble is he in now?"

Zoom followed Maria's footsteps to the library. They ended at a bookcase. There was a light coming from a space on the shelf where a book had been. It lay on the table.

Zoom climbed up onto the book and looked into the bookcase.

"This must be the way," he said.

At the back of the bookshelf a flight of stairs spiraled down into darkness. The stairway was made entirely of books!

Down and down the stairway curled. Zoom was a little bit frightened. Then he heard something that cheered him up — the sound of water lapping against stone.

Zoom found himself on a levee by a dark river. There were old crates piled everywhere, dusty and cobwebby. He chose an empty one his size, found a stick for a paddle, and pushed himself out onto the water.

"If there's trouble," thought Zoom, "Maria might need some help."

Zoom dipped his paddle into the oily waters. The current pulled him along the river's winding course. The air grew warmer.

"Brrrp! Brrrp!"

He heard something croaking.

Swooooosh!

Bats!

He saw a log. A log with eyes.

Then Zoom's crate began to spin, around and around, caught in the rapids, pulling him faster and faster.

Whooooosh!

Zoom closed his eyes and hung on tight.

Thump!

He banged into a stone dock.

He wasn't hurt. Carefully he climbed from his crate into a room aglow with torches. The walls were crawling with pictures, and all the pictures were of cats. There were cats on the ceiling, cats carved out of stone, their eyes twinkling jewels. And everywhere around him there were cloth-covered catlike shapes.

"Mummies," thought Zoom. "This must be Egypt!"

He had always wanted to go to Egypt. But where was the desert? Where were the pyramids? And most of all, where was the mighty Nile? The dark little river seemed to end at this room.

Boom! Boom! Boom!

Drums. Someone was coming.

Zoom froze. At the end of the room two enormous stone cats stood sentinel on either side of a huge stone slab. As Zoom watched, one of the stone cats raised its paw. Slowly.

Then there was a loud creaking and rumbling. The slab creaked open. A procession marched into the room — cats in hats bearing a mummy on a litter.

"Bisso, Bubastis, Bastet," chanted the cat with the tallest hat.

"Bisso, Bubastis, Bastet," the other cats answered. They placed the mummy on the floor, and then —

Boom! Boom! Boom!

They were gone, just like that. The slab closed after them.

Thud.

"Phew! That was close," whispered Zoom.

He looked at the new mummy. It was much bigger than the other mummies and the shape looked awfully familiar. Zoom felt queasy inside. Then the mummy moved.

"Get me out of here," cried a muffled but very familiar voice.

"Don't worry," said Zoom. "I'll get you out."

His pruning shears were in his coat pocket!

It didn't take him long to cut the mummy open. Maria!

"Am I glad to see you!" she said.

Maria gave Zoom a big hug. Then she began to snoop around the room. Zoom's heart sank. "Are you looking for Uncle Roy?" he asked.

"That's right," said Maria.

Zoom stared into the gloom. None of the mummies moved.

"I guess we're too late," he mumbled. Maria did not hear him.

"Aha!" she said, picking up something shiny from the cold stone floor. A silver button.

Zoom recognized it right away. "It's from Uncle Roy's captain's uniform," he said with dismay.

"Right again," said Maria.

Zoom had never felt so sad in his life. "I wonder which mummy he is?" he said.

To his surprise, Maria laughed. "Captain Roy, a mummy? I doubt it!"

"You mean," said Zoom, "he got away?"

Maria nodded. "And he left us a clue," she said, holding up the button.

Zoom jumped for joy.

"We're on the right track," said Maria. "Now if we could just get out of this catacomb."

"I think I know the way," said Zoom.

He walked to the end of the room, to the stone sentinel cats. He pushed on the cat's paw with all his might. Finally, there was a loud creaking and rumbling. The slab opened.

"Yahoo!" cried Maria.

"Where now?" asked Zoom.

"Look for buttons," said Maria.

They found themselves in a cavernous hallway lined with towering, glowering cats, whose eyes followed them as they hurried along. Zoom tried to keep his own eyes on the ground.

Boom! Boom! Boom!

The sound of the drums echoed off the walls. Were they behind or up ahead? Zoom couldn't tell.

Then he saw silver. The second button. Maria found the third.

Boom! Boom! Boom!

Were the drums getting closer?

Left, then right, Zoom and Maria followed the clues. Four, five, six, seven — ah!

Suddenly they burst out of the murky tomb onto a pier under a gentle Egyptian night. A rowboat awaited them, something silver on the seat glinting in the starlight.

"The last button," said Maria as she and Zoom clambered on board. Maria took up the oars. Zoom made his way to the bow. Far ahead he could see a clipper sitting under a crescent moon.

"The Catship!" he cried.

The rowboat sped out onto the wide black river. The mighty Nile. Zoom watched as the Catship loomed nearer and nearer. He heard a concertina and someone singing.

Then —

"Ahoy! Hurrah! Halloo!"

And there was the dark side of the ship and a rope ladder and, reaching down with a smile on his face, a large yellow tomcat in a captain's hat.

Uncle Roy.

"Welcome aboard," he said. "And just in time for a bowl of grog."

Zoom couldn't speak for smiling.

"We've got quite the trip ahead of us," said Roy.

"Where to?" asked Zoom.

"Upstream," said Captain Roy. "To search for the source of the Nile. Are you game, my small friend?"

"Yes," said Zoom.

Zoom

Tim Wynne-Jones • Eric Beddows

Zoom is an extraordinary cat. He loves adventure, and in this imaginative, beautifully illustrated anthology, he goes on a journey to the sea, an expedition to the North Pole and a trip to Egypt. These three classic picture books by award-winning author and illustrator duo Tim Wynne-Jones and Eric Beddows were highly praised when they were first published. Now young children can enjoy all of Zoom's amazing adventures in this handsome gift edition.

Zoom at Sea

". . . the tale gradually captivates the reader as the mystery and magic build and recede, like waves on the shore. A thoroughly satisfying book. — *Horn Book*

"Beddows's intricately detailed black-and-white drawings convey just the right sense of mystery as the world created by both author and illustrator seems to hover tantalizingly between reality and fantasy, and the plucky hero has an adventure any child would envy." — *Publishers Weekly*

". . . the most completely satisfying Canadian picture book ever produced." — Michele Landsberg, *Toronto Star*

~ Amelia Frances Howard-Gibbon Illustrator's Award
~ Ruth Schwartz Children's Book Award
~ IODE Book Award
~ Canada Council Award Finalist (text)

Zoom Away

". . . brilliantly executed..." — *Globe and Mail*

"The text captures the essence of a child's imagination, while the black-and-white illustrations add charm and humor." — *Horn Book*

~ Amelia Frances Howard-Gibbon Illustrator's Award

Zoom Upstream

". . . the intricate pictures are both wildly imaginative and full of minute particulars . . ." — *Booklist*

"Peppered with mystery and whimsy, intriguing black-and-white illustrations enhance the text." — *Horn Book*

"Tim Wynne-Jones's text is as witty and subtle as Eric Beddows's monochrome drawings. In both text and illustrations, the everyday and the extraordinary blend as seamlessly as the confluence of two rivers." — *Quill & Quire*

~ Governor General's Literary Award Finalist (illustration)
~ Mr. Christie's Children's Illustration Award Finalist

TIM WYNNE-JONES (www.timwynne-jones.com) is one of Canada's foremost children's writers. The author of more than two dozen books, he is a two-time winner of the Governor General's Award, four-time winner of the CLA Book of the Year Award, as well as the recipient of many other prizes and honors, including the Arthur Ellis Award, the Edgar Award, the Boston Globe-Horn Book Award and the Vicky Metcalf Award for a Body of Work.

Tim is on the faculty of Vermont College of Fine Arts.

He lives in Perth, Ontario.

ERIC BEDDOWS is a renowned illustrator who has won many awards, including the Governor General's Award for *The Rooster's Gift*, the Amelia Frances Howard-Gibbon Award for the Zoom books, and the International Ezra Jack Keats Award bronze medal. He has also had numerous one-man shows of his artwork.

He lives in Stratford, Ontario.